W9-BEA-973

ZANE D. EVANS

STAR WARS®

PHONICS
READING PROGRAM

10 stories inside!

Jedi Adventures

By Quinlan Lee

SCHOLASTIC, INC.

ISBN 978-0-545-52013-3

Published by Scholastic Inc., 557 Broadway, New York, NY 10012. Scholastic and associated logos are trademarks and/or registered trademarks of Scholastic Inc.

12 11 10 9 8 7 6 5 4 3 2 1 13 14 15 16 17/0

Printed in Singapore 46
This edition first printing, January 2013

Welcome to the **Star Wars**® Phonics Reading Program!

Learning to read is so important for your child's success in school and in life. Now **Star Wars**® is here to help your child learn important phonics skills.

Phonics is the fundamental skill of knowing that the letters we read represent the sounds we hear and say. **Star Wars**® helps your child LEARN to read and LOVE to read!

Here's how these readers work:

- At first you may want to read the story to your child.
- 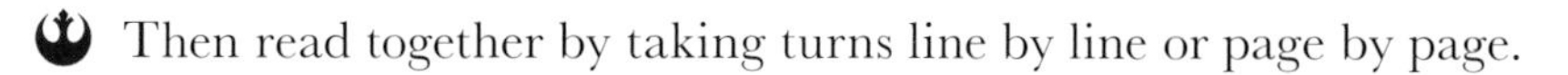
Then read together by taking turns line by line or page by page.
-  Encourage your child to read the story independently.
-  Look for all the words that have the sound being featured in the reader. Read them over and over again.

Scholastic has been encouraging young readers for more than 90 years. Thank you for letting us help you support your beginning reader.

Happy reading,

Francie Alexander
Chief Academic Officer, Scholastic Inc.

TABLE OF CONTENTS

STAR WARS®
PHONICS

Anakin **can** race a Podracer **fast**!
But will he **crash**?

In this book you will practice these **short a** words:

blast	**fast**	**last**
can	**flat**	**past**
crash	**land**	**sand**
fans	**lap**	**smash**

STAR WARS®
PHONICS
Book 1
short a
Meet Anakin

This is Anakin.
He lives in a **flat land**.
There is a lot of **sand**.

He **can** race a Podracer
fast!
Anakin goes **fast**,
fast, **fast**!
But **can** he win a race?

Many **fans** come to
the race.
The **fans** do not think
Anakin **can** win.

At **last** the race begins!
Anakin goes **fast**,
fast, **fast**!
He **blasts** over the **sand**.
He **blasts** over the **land**.

Anakin races **past**
the Podracers.
There are **blasts** here!

There are **blasts** there!
Will Anakin **crash**?

Many Podracers go
too **fast**!
Many Podracers **crash**!

They hit the **sand**.
Crash, smash, blast!

It is the **last lap**.
Can Anakin win the race?
Will he **smash**?

Anakin does not **crash**.
He wins the race!

Chewie and Han are **best** friends to the **end**.

In this book you will practice these **short e** words:

best	**jet**	**steps**
end	**left**	**tell**
get	**lend**	**yells**
help		

STAR WARS®

PHONICS

Book 2
short e

Friends to the End

This is Chewie and Han.
They do not look
the same.
They do not talk
the same.
But they are **best** friends.

Han flies the ship.
Chewie **helps** him.

They **jet** right!
They **jet** **left**!

Sometimes they need to
get away fast, fast, fast.
Chewie **steps** up to **help**.

They **jet** away.
Zoom!

Sometimes the ship
will not **jet**.
Who can **help** Han fix it?
Chewie can **lend** a hand.

Sometimes Chewie **yells**,
"Rrr, Rrr, Rrr!"
Who can **tell** what
Chewie says?
Han can **tell**!

Sometimes Chewie
gets stuck.
He needs **help** to
get out.
He needs a friend.

Friends **help** each other in good times.

Friends **help** each other in bad times.

Chewie and Han
are **best** friends
to the **end**.

The Jedi are on a **trip**.

Watch out! A **big fish zips** after the **ship**.

In this book you will practice these **short i** words:

big	**grins**	**skip**
fins	**it**	**trip**
fish	**lips**	**yips**
flips	**ship**	**zip**

Jar Jar's Trip

The Jedi must take a **trip**.

They need a **ship**.

The Jedi get a **ship**.
They also get Jar Jar.

Jar Jar wants to **skip** the **trip**.

The **ship** goes **zip**, **zip**, **zip**.
The **ship zips** through the water.

Little **fish zip** through the water, too.

A **big** red **fish** sees
the **ship**.
It has **big fins**.

It has **big**, **big lips**.
The **fish zips**
after the **ship**.

The **big fish** gets the **ship**.

The **big fish flips** the **ship** around.

"This **trip** is bad,"
yips Jar Jar.

The **big fish** drops
the **ship**.

The **ship zips** away.

Jar Jar **grins**.
"This **trip** is not so bad,"
he says.

The **Ewoks** are **not** big.
But that does **not stop** them.

In this book you will practice these **short o** words:

drop	**log**	**rock**
Ewoks	**lot**	**stop**
hop	**not**	**top**

STAR WARS®

PHONICS

Book 4
short o

Here Come the Ewoks

The **Ewoks** are **not** big.
But that does **not**
stop them.

Ewoks live in **rock**
and **log** huts.
The huts are **not** big.
The huts are on **top**
of trees!

Ewoks use ropes to get
to the **top**.
They **hop** up, up, up
to the **top**.
Then they **drop** back
down.

Ewoks like traps.
Traps go up, up, up
to the **top**.
But traps do **not drop**
back down.

Ewoks trap Luke, Han, and C-3PO.

They let C-3PO go.
They like C-3PO a **lot**.

The **Ewoks** do **not** let
Luke and Han go.
"**Stop**!" C-3PO says.
Now the **Ewoks** let
them go.
"Thanks a **lot**," Han says.

Now the **Ewoks** are
friends with Han
and Luke.
The **Ewoks** like
them a **lot**.

The **Ewoks** are **not** big.
But that does **not stop**
them.
They will win!

A Jedi **must** learn to **trust** the Force.

In this book you will practice these **short u** words:

duck	**must**	**trust**
cut	**run**	**up**
jump		

STAR WARS®
PHONICS
Book 5
short u
How to Be a Jedi

Being a Jedi is hard.

A Jedi **must** learn a lot.

A Jedi **must** be strong.
A Jedi **must** be fast.

A Jedi will need help.

So a Jedi learns to **trust** his friends.

A Jedi will not always win.

So a Jedi learns to not give **up**.

A Jedi will need his saber.
So a Jedi learns
to spin and **duck**.
And a Jedi learns
to **jump** and **cut**.

A Jedi **must** use the Force.

The Force will help
a Jedi **duck** and **cut**.

The Force will help
a Jedi **jump**.
The Force will help
a Jedi **run**.

Most of all, a Jedi **must** learn to **trust** the Force.

Luke and Leia are in a **chase**.
This is not a **safe race**!

In this book you will practice these **long a** words:

brakes	**race**	**shake**
chase	**saber**	**take**
fakes	**safe**	

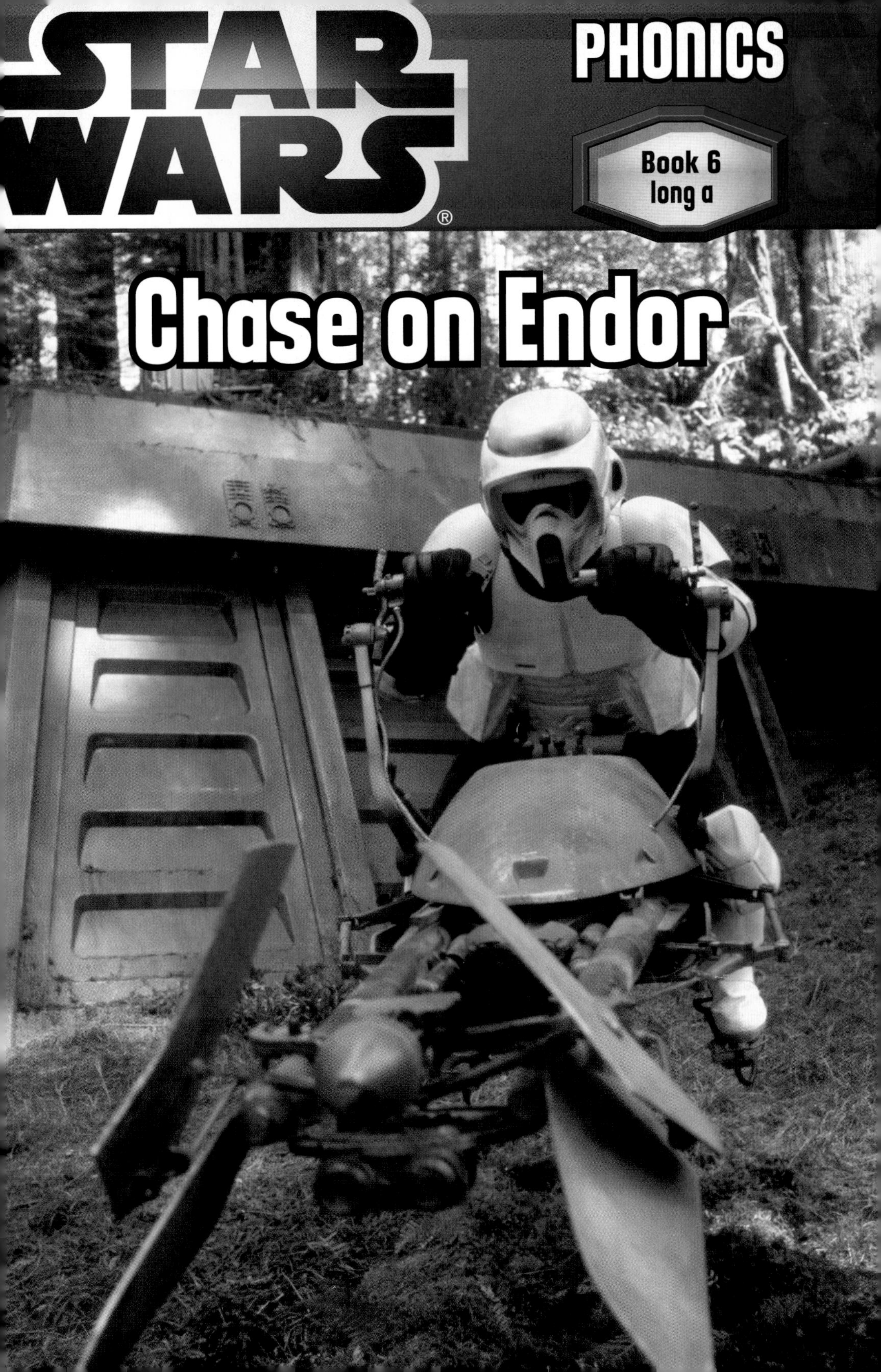
STAR WARS®
PHONICS
Book 6
long a
Chase on Endor

Luke **takes** off.
Leia **takes** off.

The trooper **takes** off.
The **chase** is on!

They **race** fast,
fast, faster!
Luke **fakes** left.
Luke **fakes** right.

Luke cannot **shake**
the trooper.

The trooper **takes** a hit!
Luke **races** past him.

More troopers join
the **chase**.
They **race** after Leia.
They **race** after Luke.

Luke hits the **brakes**.
He blasts the **racer**.
Take that, Trooper!

Oh, no! Leia **takes** a hit!
She goes down.
But she is **safe**.

Luke jumps off his **racer**.
He **takes** out his **saber**.
The trooper **races**
to Luke.

Take that, Trooper!
The **chase** is over.

Obi-Wan and Luke **need** a ship with **speed**.
Han has the ship they **need**!

In this book you will practice vowel combinations that together make the **long e** sound.

creep **meet** **speed**
fleet **need**
free **see**

Meet Han Solo

Obi-Wan and Luke
need to **speed** away.
They **need** a ship.

Obi-Wan **meets** Chewie.
Does he have the ship
they **need**?
No.

Luke **meets** a **creep**.
Does he have the ship
they **need**?
No.

Obi-Wan and Luke
meet Han.
Han has the ship
they **need**!
But ships are not **free**.

“What do you **need**?”
Obi-Wan asks.

Han **needs** money.
Han **needs** lots of money.

Obi-Wan has a lot
of money.
But Obi-Wan **needs**
a ship with **speed**.
Can Han's ship **speed**?

Yes, Han's ship
can **speed**!
It is fast.
It is the fastest in
the **fleet**.
They make a deal.

"It was good to **meet**
Han," says Obi-Wan.
"We will **see**," says Luke.

Han and Leia need to **hide**. Lando says he can help. But is Lando **nice**? Or is he **slime**?

In this book you will practice these **long i** words:

hide **nice** **slime**

likes **side** **time**

mine

STAR WARS®
PHONICS
Book 8
long i
Hide Out

Han and Leia need
to **hide**.

They need **time**
to fix the ship.

They meet Lando.
Lando is **nice**.
Han **likes** him.
Leia **likes** him.

Lando helps them **hide**.
“I am on your **side**,”
says Lando.
But is he on their **side**?

No! Lando is not
on their **side**.
He let Darth Vader
hide, too!

“Han is **mine**!”
Darth Vader says.
“No one can **hide**
from me.”

No one **likes** Vader.
Now no one **likes** Lando.
"But I am on your **side**,"
says Lando.

“You are not on our **side**!” Leia says.

"You are **slime**!"

Is Lando really **slime**?
Only **time** will tell.

Obi-Wan finds the **home** of the **clones**.
Will the **clones** be friend or **foe**?

In this book you will practice three patterns that make the **long o** sound.

clone	**hello**	**so**
code	**home**	**told**
foe	**hopes**	**zone**
go		

STAR WARS®

PHONICS

Book 9
long o

Here Come the Clones

Obi-Wan is on a trip.
He is far from **home**.

Obi-Wan finds the **home** of the **clones**.

He will **go** inside.

The **clone** maker says,
“**Hello**, Jedi.”

"The **clones** are ready to **go**!"

The **clone** maker **hopes**
Obi-Wan will like the
clones.
Obi-Wan asks,
"How many **clones** are
there?"

Obi-Wan goes to the
clone zone.
There are **so** many
clones!
Clones, **clones**,
everywhere!

The **clone** maker has
a **code**.
The **code** makes all
the **clones** the same.

The **clone** maker says,
“The **clones** are ready
to fight.
Clones will do what
they are **told**.”

But will the **clones**
be friend or **foe**?

A Jedi can **use** the Force.
Will **Luke** be a Jedi, too?

In this book you will practice two patterns that make the **long u** sound.

dunes **rescue** **use**

Luke **true**

STAR WARS®

PHONICS

Book 10
long u

Use the Force, Luke!

Luke lives in
the sand **dunes**.
It is hot.
It is windy.
Luke does not like it.

Luke does not know
the truth.
His dad was a Jedi.
A Jedi can **use** the Force.
Will **Luke** be a Jedi, too?

Luke meets Obi-Wan.
Obi-Wan is a Jedi.
Obi-Wan can **use**
the Force.

Obi-Wan helps **Luke**
leave the **dunes**.

Obi-Wan helps **Luke**
become a Jedi.
He teaches **Luke**
to **use** the Force.

It is time for **Luke**
to **use** the Force.
Is **Luke** ready?

Leia needs a **rescue**.
Can **Luke use** the Force?
Yes!
Luke rescues Leia!

Now **Luke** is a **true** Jedi.

STAR WARS®

STAR WARS